The Adventures of Flemming

JANICE DEAN
SUSAN HENSON
PAM MASHBURN
KIMBERLY SHEPPARD

illustrated by
KAREN CRAFT

This book belongs to......

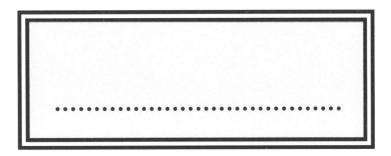

This story is about a friendly snake named Flemming
who is lost in Canada and ends up finding
the best friend he has ever had.

The Flemming Adventures......
Lost in Canada

Dedicated to the Bethany Baptist Canadian Mission Team, our brothers and sisters in Christ and our friends from Cambrian Heights in Calgary, Alberta Canada.

Thanks to our families and friends for their support and encouragement along the journey. Karen Craft...you are awesome. You were able to take the words and make them come to life. You knew what we wanted even when we didn't. Thanks for using the talent God has given you. Bro. Al, you are a great cheerleader—many thanks. We appreciate your support. Linda Dunsmore, thanks for the time you took to edit our many versions. Fred Rainer, your technical expertise sealed the deal.

ENDORSEMENTS

"This is a great tool for ministry with children, especially unchurched children. The message is very simple and extremely clear, as well as being professionally written." **DK Hale Church Support Ministry Leader Canadian National Baptist Convention**

This team of missionaries from Bethany Baptist Church in McDonough, Georgia are totally sold out to Jesus. They are what I call FAT Christians and that is Faithful, Available, and Teachable. They came to Cambrian Heights Baptist Church in Calgary, Alberta, Canada and demonstrated flexibility. After reading this incredible little book about a snake's adventures to find his way in Canada I would say that the book is at least one of the best reads I have ever enjoyed. It is written with purpose and for children. It is the best child evangelism presentation to date. I think it should be animated. My personal favorite character is Mr. B. Go ahead read and see if you don't love him also. **Reverend Dwayne R. Bartley, Retired pastor, Calgary, Alberta**

"The Flemming Adventures" is a wonderful simplistic method of sharing the gospel with children. The book is written by four dedicated Christian women who have a heart for child evangelism and missions. It is my joy to be their pastor." **Al O'Quinn, Senior Pastor, Bethany Baptist Church, McDonough, Georgia**

"The Flemming Adventures" is a wonderfully crafted narrative that will inspire readers young and old to be passionate about being on mission for God. **Barry Saunders,** Children's Pastor, **Bethany Baptist Church, McDonough, Georgia**

Flemming takes children on a Canadian journey from lostness to salvation in a unique and interesting way any child can understand.   This book will be ideal for parents to prepare their children to experience salvation for themselves and may answer those spiritual questions your children are asking about Jesus and salvation. **Dr. C. Michael Gravette, Specialist Mission Volunteers Ministries Georgia Baptist Convention, Duluth, GA**

"A cool book with lots of funny characters! It was interesting and awesome!"
Jake - 8 years old, McDonough, Georgia

The Adventures of Flemming is a very unique and interesting story detailing the simple plan of salvation for kids. It makes the ABC's of salvation come to life. I read the story to my kids in Good News Club last year. Now, they are eagerly waiting to see where Flemming's next adventure takes him. **Shirley Rainer, Good News Club Coordinator, Unity Grove Elementary, McDonough, Georgia**

Even though it was summer, the weather was still chilly in Canada. "Brrrrrrrr," Flemming shivered and thought to himself, "I sure could use a nap but I need to find a warm place." Looking around, he spotted some boxes and slithered over to check them out. "Hmmmm... I think this will do."

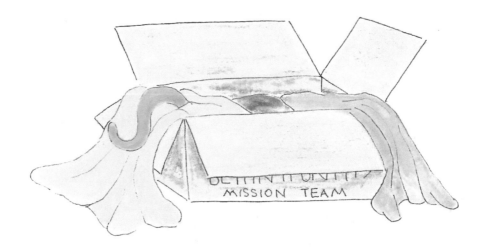

Flemming stuck his little green head underneath the blankets in the box. "Yes," he thought, "this is just perfect."

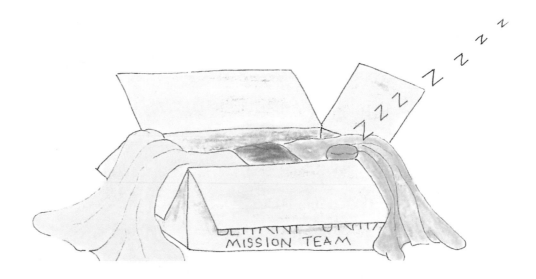

Warm and cozy, Flemming quickly fell sound asleep.

Our sleeping Flemming was on an adventure and didn't even know it! You see, the boxes were loaded onto a bus taking the Bethany Mission Team to Calgary, Alberta. They are going to help their friends in Calgary build a church.

The humming of the bus motor kept Flemming lulled to sleep for a long time, but when the bus stopped, Flemming woke up. He slowly opened his eyes, stretched his scaly neck as tall as he could and stuck his head out of the box. There were people running around laughing and smiling here in Calgary but not poor Flemming. "Uh oh," Flemming thought, feeling a little sick, "this isn't the place where I crawled into this box. Where am I?"

Flemming slithered up and out of the box and down the side of the bus. "What now?" Flemming wondered as he slithered down the road. "Where am I and what am I going to do?"

Flemming came to a fork in the road. He spotted a sign and wiggled up the post to get a closer look. WIDE? or NARROW? Which way should he go? Flemming glanced toward the Narrow path. It was lined with tall trees that cast shadows on the path. It looked a little dark and scary. In front of him was the Wide path and it was bright with sunshine. "Sunshine is good," Flemming thought. "I'll take the Wide path"... and off he went.

Just a short distance down the Wide path, Flemming spotted a black bird sitting on a rock with his wings over his eyes. The bird seemed to be talking to someone but no one was there! Flemming slithered up to the black bird and cleared his throat, "Ahem, excuse me, who are you and who are you talking to?" The bird, a little startled, opened his eyes wide and replied, "Why I'm Roy, the Praying Magpie, and I was talking to Jesus." "Who is Jesus?" Flemming wanted to know.

Roy was about to tell Flemming all about Jesus when a Foxote came trotting down the path. Seeing Flemming, he stopped and exclaimed, "Now just what do we have here? I've never seen anything like you before!"

"I'm Flemming, a long, scaly snake and I'm lost!" Flemming hissed. Circling above them, Roy interrupted, "and I was just about to tell Flemming all about Jesus and pray to ask Jesus to help Flemming find his way."

"Well, I'm Casey," said the Foxote with a sneer, "I think you're weird. You have no legs. How do you walk?" Poor Flemming. He felt so alone. No one ever liked him. People ran from him, and now he didn't know where to go or what to do.

Flemming had
had a very long day.
He was lost and now this
Foxote was making fun of him--
it was just more than he could take!
Flemming stretched himself as tall as he
could get and gave a big H-i-s-s-s-s-s-s-s-s-s-
to the Foxote. "Well, I never!" exclaimed
Casey, the Foxote, and tucking his tail,
turned and scurried down the path.

Sad and lonely, Flemming slithered down the Wide path. He was thinking about all that had happened to him today, so he was really startled when he looked up and was staring into a big brown nose! Raising his eyes, he hissed timidly, "h-i-s-s-s-s. I'm Flemming and I'm lost. Can you help me find my way?" The big nose took a step back, and Flemming realized it was attached to the biggest animal he had ever seen. "W-w-w-w-what are you?" Flemming hissed in a whisper. With a big snort and a chuckle, the big nose replied, "I'm a mule deer, little fella, and you can call me CD. I believe what you want is up ahead. Just follow the path. You'll come to a bridge, and from there you should be able to find your way."

It wasn't long before Flemming's journey was interrupted again. Roy, the Praying Magpie swooped down onto the path in front of Flemming. "What are you doing here?" he asked.

Flemming explained, "CD, the mule deer told me I would find my way following this path." Roy, the Praying Magpie just shook his head, "CD didn't tell you about praying to Jesus for help? Jesus knows everything and everyone. Jesus will always help you find your way. Jesus can do anything." Flemming was tired and confused. "But Roy, what is praying?" he asked. Roy motioned for Flemming to come closer. Roy bowed his head, closed his eyes and began talking softly. Flemming still wasn't sure who Roy was talking to, but since Roy's eyes were closed, Flemming was pretty sure it wasn't him. However, he liked the kindness in Roy's voice when he did this thing called praying. When Roy was quiet again, he opened his eyes and looked at Flemming. "I think you will find the right path soon, my friend," and with that Roy flew away.

Just as Flemming was about to ask more about this praying thing, he heard a buzzing sound and felt a terrible sting on the top of his head. "Ouuuuuuch!" Flemming hissed with a start. Looking up he saw the biggest insect he had ever seen. "Bzzzzzzzzz.....Bzzzzzzzzzz, I'm Big D, a Canadian Mosquito, and Roy the Praying Magpie is right! You're not on the right path!"

"But I'm on the Wide path just like CD, the Mule Deer, suggested," Flemming replied. "Besides, how can I be taking the wrong path when I really don't know where I'm going?" Big D just threw up both hands and Bzzzzzzzzzzed away.

Left all alone again, Flemming slithered down the path. He was thinking about this praying thing again when a fluffy rabbit came hopping b-o-i-n-g b-o-i-n-g out of the tall grass. "Hey! Not so fast!" Flemming called after the rabbit. "My name is Flemming. I'm lost and I really need your help. Where are you going?" The rabbit turned and hopped b-o-i-n-g b-o-i-n-g back toward Flemming. "Sorry! My name is O.Q. and I'm sort of in a hurry. I'm on my way to church." "What is church?" Flemming asked. "Will it help me find my way?" Hopping in place, O.Q. replied, "Church is where we all go on Sunday, but I don't have time to wait for you today."

All alone again,
Flemming just dropped
his head and sighed.

Roy, the Praying Magpie, was nearby. Swooping down, he landed with a loud plop in front of Flemming. "Oh, Roy, boy am I glad to see you!" Flemming hissed. "Have you talked to that Jesus again so I'll know which is the right path?" "Yes, as a matter of fact, I have," Roy replied. He waddled to the edge of the path and pointed his wing. "Come this way. The right path is just up ahead. Look, there is a bridge in the distance where you can cross over. Then you will be on the right path." As Roy, the Praying Magpie, flew away, Flemming was still happily hissing, "Thank you, Roy, thank you!"

Flemming
was getting excited
as he reached the bridge. He slithered
over the top and was making his way down the
other side when he met a tall work horse galloping
down the path. "Hi, I'm Flemming," he hissed. "I'm
lost and can't find my way. Is this the right path?"
"Welp," the horse replied, "that depends. I'm Mr. B
and whether this is the right path or not depends
on where you're aheadin'." "Oh no, . . .here we
go again," Flemming hissed, " Mr. B, I'll tell you
like I told Roy, the Praying Magpie, and Casey, the
Foxote, and CD, the Mule Deer, and Big D, the
Canadian Mosquito, and O.Q., the Rabbit.... I'M
LOST AND I CAN'T FIND MY WAY!"

Mr. B let out a deep horsey sigh and began trotting
down the path. Looking over his shoulder he
called to Flemming, "I'm on my way to learn about
someone that can help.

I think we take this path right here along the creek. You can come with us if you like. My friend, Benje, the Mouse, was just telling me about the right path. Speak up, Benje, our new friend Flemming wants to hear too!"

Slithering along next to Mr. B, Flemming cautiously eyed Benje who was sitting on Mr. B's back. "Most mice don't like me. In fact, they run from me," Flemming hissed. "Don't worry," Benje said looking down at Flemming, "I'm not afraid of you. I have a Protector." Confused, Flemming looked around. "I don't see anyone protecting you," he hissed to Benje. Benje smiled, "His name is Jesus. You can't see him because He's in my heart." "Oh not again!" Flemming thought, "Not that Jesus thing again! Just who is Jesus exactly?" he asked. "Why, he's my best friend, said Benje. "He is with me all the time. Just because you don't see Him, doesn't mean He's not here."

"Look! Benje said, pointing up ahead. "We're almost there! You can learn a lot about Jesus when we get there." "Get where?" Flemming asked. "To church, silly!" Benje said with a smile. "You'll like everyone there, and I'm sure they will like you." "I don't think so," Flemming thought to himself. "No one ever likes a long, scaly snake."

Arriving at this place called church, Mr. B, Benje and Flemming were met by Kimberly. She had arrived earlier on a bus with the mission team from her church in Georgia. The mission team was helping build a new addition to the Calgary church. Kimberly put down the tools and welcomed her new friends.

Flemming was so surprised when Kimberly didn't act afraid of him. Kimberly invited them to the welcome center. Everyone there was smiling. Flemming wondered what made the entire Calgary church group so happy. Flemming slithered up to Kimberly, "Can you please tell me why everyone here is so friendly and happy?" Kimberly bent down and smiled. No one had ever smiled at Flemming like that. "Flemming," said Kimberly, "we have Jesus in our hearts and we follow him every day. That's why I'm here working on the new addition. Many people have accepted Jesus into their hearts and are coming to church, so our friends in Calgary need more space." "Kimberly," Flemming hissed softly, "please tell me more about this Jesus and how I can get Him into my heart too."

It's not hard to understand," said Kimberly. "It's as easy as ABC. The first thing you have to do is.........

 **A**DMIT that you're a sinner or that you have done unkind things. "Well, that's easy for me," Flemming said. "I've done a lot of unkind things. Then what?"

 **B**ELIEVE that Jesus died on the cross for your sins and then came back again after three days," said Kimberly. "Wow," said Flemming, "you mean someone would do that for me?" "Yes," Kimberly replied. "In the Bible, John 3:16 says that God loved us so much that He gave us Jesus, His only Son, to die for our sins." "I didn't think anyone loved me," said Flemming, "Then what?"

 **C**OMMIT your life to Him. "Commit?" Flemming asked. "It means giving your life to Jesus and telling Him that everything you do is for Him," Kimberly continued, "then all you have to do is ask Jesus into your heart and life, and He will stay with you forever."

"Flemming would you like me to pray with you?" Kimberly asked. "Why sure! That's what Roy, the Praying Magpie, does all the time." As Kimberly bowed her head and closed her eyes, she reminded Flemming, "You can pray to Jesus any time you like. He will always listen."

Jesus, I admit and know that I have done many things that have displeased you.
I believe that you died on the cross for me and then came back three days later because you loved me.
I commit my life and everything that I do to you, Jesus.
I ask you to come and live in my heart and life so you will be with me always.
In Jesus' name, I pray.
Amen.

When Flemming opened his eyes, he felt different. If only he had legs, he would jump up and down. Everyone made a circle around him. When he looked around, he saw many of the creatures and people that he had met that day. There next to Kimberly was Roy, the Praying Magpie, and O.Q., the Rabbit, and Casey Foxote and CD, the Mule Deer, and Big D, the Canadian Mosquito, and even Mr. B and Benje. Flemming didn't think he could be any happier. For the first time, Flemming had real friends. They invited him to Sunday School where they study the Bible and learn more about Jesus.

Flemming was so excited that he wanted to tell everyone about Jesus, his new best friend. Kimberly said, "You can tell all your friends and family. You can tell everyone you meet." Flemming was invited to go on the next mission trip, and this time Kimberly told him he *didn't have to ride in a box*! Just then Roy, the Praying Magpie, and all Flemming's other new friends began singing a song called *Jesus Loves Me*. After the first verse, a very happy Flemming hissed along and for the first time. . .no one made fun of him.

Where in the world will Flemming go next?

The ABC's of Salvation

ADMIT **that you're a sinner or that you have done unkind things and turn from them. In the Bible, Romans 3:23 tells us that everyone has sinned and does unkind things. No one is perfect but God.**

BELIEVE that Jesus died on the cross for your sins and then came back again after three days. In the Bible, **John 3:16** says that God loved us so much that He gave us **Jesus**, His only Son, to die for our sins.

COMMIT your life to Him. **Commit** means giving your life to Jesus and telling Him that everything you do is for Him. In the Bible, **Romans 10:9** tells us to confess Jesus with our mouth and believe in our heart and we will be saved. It's that easy. **Ask** Jesus into your heart and life, and He will stay with you forever.

CPSIA information can be obtained at www.ICGtesting.com

224529LV00004B